For Paul and Kirstie, Suede and Molly
- D.C.

For Hugh on the Upper Feeny Mountain
- B.O'D.

For my own wee banshee
- K.B.

First published in Ireland by Discovery Publications,
Brookfield Business Centre, 333 Crumlin Road, Belfast BT14 7EA
Telephone: 028 9049 2410
Email address: declan.carville@ntlworld.com

Text © 2002 Declan Carville

Book Design © 2002 Bernard O'Donnell

Illustrations © 2002 Kieron Black

A CIP catalogue record of this book is available from the British Library.

Printed in Ireland by Graham & Heslip.

ISBN 0-9538222-5-7

1 2 3 4 5 6 7 8 9 10

Boo!!! said the banshee

Declan Carville

illustrated by Kieron Black

book design by Bernard O' Donnell

Oonagh

was a banshee from a quiet little spot in deepest, darkest Ireland.

In this part of the world the countryside was very barren. A few farms, a few cottages scattered here and there. Not much else really.

Wait a minute - did anyone hear a scream?

Oonagh lived underground with her relations - all 35 of them.
At times, not surprisingly, it could get very crowded.

Now the banshees did have a special tradition. In many ways, they
were very traditional people. Every night, on the stroke of
midnight (or thereabouts) they all went out to spook. Everybody.
Not just the ladies - because banshees are female you know. In fact,
this was more like a military operation. Her younger brothers were
often the worst. Quite a handful and off like a shot once the signal
was given.
"Not so loud," scolded Grandma Kelly. "You have my head tormented
and we're not even over the door yet!"

Oonagh, however, was different to the others. She hated the thought of leaving the house, especially after dark. She was always the last in line.

"Tell that daughter of yours to get a move on," Uncle Cornelius would say.

"But she's only a youngster," replied her mother, trying to defend the young girl.

"What planet are you on, Briege?" protested Aunty Sally. "She's 103 next birthday!"

And so it was.

One night, however, in the middle of winter, darkness arrived earlier than usual. The young ones were watching their favourite movie - The Addams Family - when Aunty Eileen suddenly entered the room at such speed even the carpet seemed to raise off the floor.

"Hocus pocus one two three, ready for some fun? - then follow me!!!!"
Aunty Eileen said everything in rhyme.
"Thank heavens for that," muttered Aunty Nora, throwing her knitting in the air. "I've been bored rigid in here all day."

"But the movie..." said Oonagh, "it's not over yet."
Nobody was listening. Aunty Maggie was hunting high and low for a pair of her favourite winter gloves while Oonagh's brothers and sisters were pushing against each other as they scrambled towards the door. It was one thing to watch a scary movie, but to play a part in your very own was hard to resist.
"Patience, patience, you little minx," said Grandma Kelly, grabbing hold of young Attracta from behind.

Uncle Kevin had been planning ahead. He made all the arrangements. He loved to do that. He even wore a hat. The banshees were going to sweep over the hills to a lonely lake in the middle of the mountains, home to some beautiful white swans. Uncle Kevin had been secretly watching them.

Poor Oonagh. Her stomach turned to knots. It was bad enough that it was pitch dark but if one of her brothers or sisters got over excited, as usually happened, she could end up in the lake herself. Cold, dark and wet. It didn't bear thinking about. But before she knew it, they were off.

"Come along, Oonagh," urged her mother from somewhere in the darkness. "Stay close by me and you'll not get lost."
Oonagh tried to keep up. They swept over the hills and mountains until at last they could see the shimmering surface of the lake in the pale winter moonlight. The white swans were dotted here and there.

"So far, so good," said Uncle Kevin in a low voice. "Now everybody take up your positions and remember everything I've told you." He adjusted his hat. "On the count of three; one... two..."

"NO!!!" shouted Oonagh. "I CAN'T DO IT!"

Everybody turned and stared. Well, almost everybody. A few of the younger banshees had been too keen and were half-way down the hillside before they realized what had happened. There was a lot of confusion.

"False alarm," shouted young Michael to his brothers and sisters.

"Who the devil was that?" asked Uncle Kevin, gazing into the darkness. "What in heavens happened there???"

"Oonagh!!!" shouted Uncle Patrick. "You've been warned before..."

"I'll not do it!!" replied Oonagh, edging away from the crowd. "You can't force me..."

"Leave her alone!" said Oonagh's mother. "She's not feeling well... She's... She's got an upset stomach. I think it was something she ate."

"Briege Brennan," interrupted Aunty Maggie, quite annoyed. "If you've got something to say about my cooking then spit it out!"

"Oonagh? Oonagh who???" asked Uncle Kevin, trying to make sense of what was going on. "Was she one of mine???"

"You stupid girl!" scolded Uncle Patrick. "You've ruined everything!"

Oonagh didn't know where to turn. All eyes were upon her and for all the wrong reasons. Close to tears, and without a moment's hesitation, she fled in the direction of home. Above the banshees and in the midst of all the turmoil, one of the beautiful white swans had taken flight into the darkened sky.

"Drat and double drat" shouted Uncle Kevin. "Doesn't that silly girl know the first rule of any attack. Never EVER let the enemy know where you are, lest they get an idea. You silly girl. Where is she anyway? Has she been with us long?" he asked, reaching for his glasses.

"She's 103 next birthday," interrupted young Attracta.

"She's my sister" said Sinead "and she's afraid of the dark."

"Afraid of the dark? Afraid of the dark?" shrieked Uncle Kevin, almost choking on his own words.

"Out in the dark, what a lark...!!!" laughed Aunty Eileen.

"What in heavens are you saying girl?" asked Uncle Kevin, "Where did she train? Not under me, I'm quite sure." He turned to face Uncle Patrick. "She must be one of yours, is she? Eh? What do you know about this then?"

The winter night was filled with the sound of banshee voices. Wailings more like. Uncle Kevin had taken off his hat while Uncle Patrick searched high and low for Oonagh. He had no hope - she was already half-way home, with her mother close behind.

"Oonagh, pet, you're going to have to do better," pleaded her mother as they reached the front door. "Uncle Kevin is furious. He's barely forgiven us for the last time we raided Farmer Tom's yard. The others will be mad. Another night wasted. We'll never hear the end of it."

"I can't face it any more," replied Oonagh. "I've had enough. I'm not doing it again. EVER."

Later that morning, as darkness turned to light, the others did start to return home. It was around seven o'clock when Oonagh's brothers and sisters tumbled into the kitchen, drained of all energy and covered in chicken feathers from head to toe. "Those children of yours, Briege Brennan, they're a complete disgrace," shouted Grandma Kelly as she stumbled through the front door, pushing the young ones aside. "Bring them to a farmyard and they don't know how to behave. But I should have known that by now. Just look at the state of this place. There's feathers everywhere in here." Her voice rose to a screeching pitch. "Get outside the lot of you and brush them off," she scolded. "YOU HAVE THIS PLACE LOOKING LIKE A HEN HOUSE!!!"

With the young ones banished outdoors, a feeling of calm returned to the little kitchen. But not for long. Grandma Kelly turned to face Oonagh and her mother. "And where did you two end up anyway?" she said. "Talk about a right useless bunch."

"We have been making plans," said Oonagh's mother. "Oonagh will tell you all about it tomorrow."

"Plans? What sort of plans?" asked Aunty Phil, pulling a handful of straw out of her hair.

"All in good time," repeated Oonagh's mother, "after you've had a good sleep."

Oonagh smiled and winked at her mother before climbing into bed.

"Useless article," murmured Grandma Kelly as she reached for a carrot.

Later that day everyone woke up at different times.

"I had the most wonderful nightmare," said young Attracta coming down the stairs, scratching her head. "The rabbits next door went down the wrong hole and ended up in here. We had great fun playing hide and seek!"

"Enough of that talk," said Aunty Maggie. "There'll be no rabbits in here. No rabbits, no pets, never. Now sit down and eat your toast."

It wasn't until breakfast was over, however, that young Joseph remarked that he hadn't seen his sister at all that day.

"Where is Oonagh?" he asked.

At that, the front door of the house swung open with such force that the wind nearly blew the sugar off the table.

"Holy Moses!!!" shrieked Aunty Maggie, raising her cup in the air. "Look what the cat's dragged in!!!"

And there was Oonagh, standing in the doorway, grinning from ear to ear.

"Just where have you been" asked Grandma Kelly "at this hour of the day? And what the dickens is that smell???" The old woman gasped in horror. "Dracula's Daughter!!! You smelly article!!! What have you been doing?"

Young Michael rushed forward to steady Aunty Cissy who was clearly overcome with the stench.

"Out of this kitchen at once!!!" wailed Grandma Kelly, rising from the table and waving her arms in the air. "Briege come here and take this daughter of yours..."

"I've been spooking" replied Oonagh, holding her head high and going nowhere. "And for your information, it's cow manure."

"Cow manure!!?" repeated Grandma Kelly. "You filthy animal!!"

"Spooking? At this time of the day?" interrupted Aunty Teasie. "What's got into the girl?"

"And why not?" replied Oonagh's mother. "Isn't a spook during the day as good as a spook at night?"

"I had a grand time," said Oonagh, "out in the fields. The cows were running everywhere!"

"My poor head," cried Grandma Kelly, close to tears and starting to shake all over. "You wicked, wicked child..."

But it was true. The cows were running everywhere. And the sheep and the pigs. Oonagh was so pleased with herself. "You lot can do as you wish," she told the other banshees, "but my time spent spooking in the dark is over!" And she screamed with delight!

Now it's a well known fact that a bump in the night can give anyone the shivers, but the same could never be said for when a cow leaps over a ditch. Take heed, therefore, to have your wits about you at all times. Even in the sleepy Irish countryside things are not always quite as they seem.

Enjoy more great picture books from Discovery Publications

The Fairy Glen

Declan Carville &
Belinda Larmour
ISBN 09538222-3-0

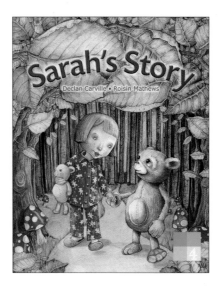

Sarah's Story

Declan Carville &
Roisin Mathews
ISBN 0-9538222-6-5

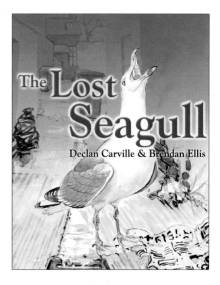

The Lost Seagull

Declan Carville &
Brendan Ellis
ISBN 0-9538222-4-9

A Day to Remember
at the Giant's Causeway

Declan Carville &
Brendan Ellis
ISBN 09538222-0-6

Valentine O'Byrne
Irish Dancer

Declan Carville &
Brendan Ellis
ISBN 09538222-1-4

The Incredible
Sister Bridget

Declan Carville &
Kieron Black
ISBN 09538222-2-2